Deserts

Yvonne Franklin

Deserts

Publishing Credits

Editorial Director
Dona Herweck Rice

Associate Editor
James Anderson

Editor-in-Chief
Sharon Coan, M.S.Ed.

Creative Director
Lee Aucoin

Illustration Manager
Timothy J. Bradley

Publisher
Rachelle Cracchiolo, M.S.Ed.

Science Consultants
Scot Oschman, Ph.D.
David W. Schroeder, M.S.

Teacher Created Materials
5301 Oceanus Drive
Huntington Beach, CA 92649-1030
http://www.tcmpub.com

ISBN 978-1-4333-0315-9

Printed by: 51497
Printed in: China

Table of Contents

Desert Music

Shhh. Be very still and listen.

Swish, swish. A long green tail swishes against the sand. Thump, thump. Strong, furry paws jump behind the shade of a cactus. Whoosh, whoosh. Long spindly legs and wings rub together. Rustle, rustle. A gentle wind blows through a low creosote (KREE-uh-soht) bush.

These are quiet sounds. You must listen very carefully. Can you hear them? They are calm and so faint that they are barely there. But the sounds are there, just as the creatures and plants that make those sounds are there.

Together, they make the music of the **desert**.

Desert

A desert is an area of very dry land with little rainfall. The area might also be a desert because of permanent frost or very little soil. Deserts may have little or no plant life. They may have few animals, as well. Still, a variety of animal **species** (SPEE-seez) can be found in many deserts.

Australian
bearded dragon
jack rabbit
creosote bush
grasshopper

Desert Ecosystems

At first glance, it may seem as though there is not much in a desert. The land may seem empty. The quiet suggests that there are few or no animals. The weather may not seem friendly to life.

But look closer. A desert is made of **ecosystems** (EK-oh-sis-tuhmz). In an ecosystem, plants, animals, land, water, and air work together. The plants and animals depend on one another. They depend on the land, water, and air, as well. An ecosystem is like a puzzle. Each piece of the puzzle is needed. Without even one piece, the puzzle is not whole.

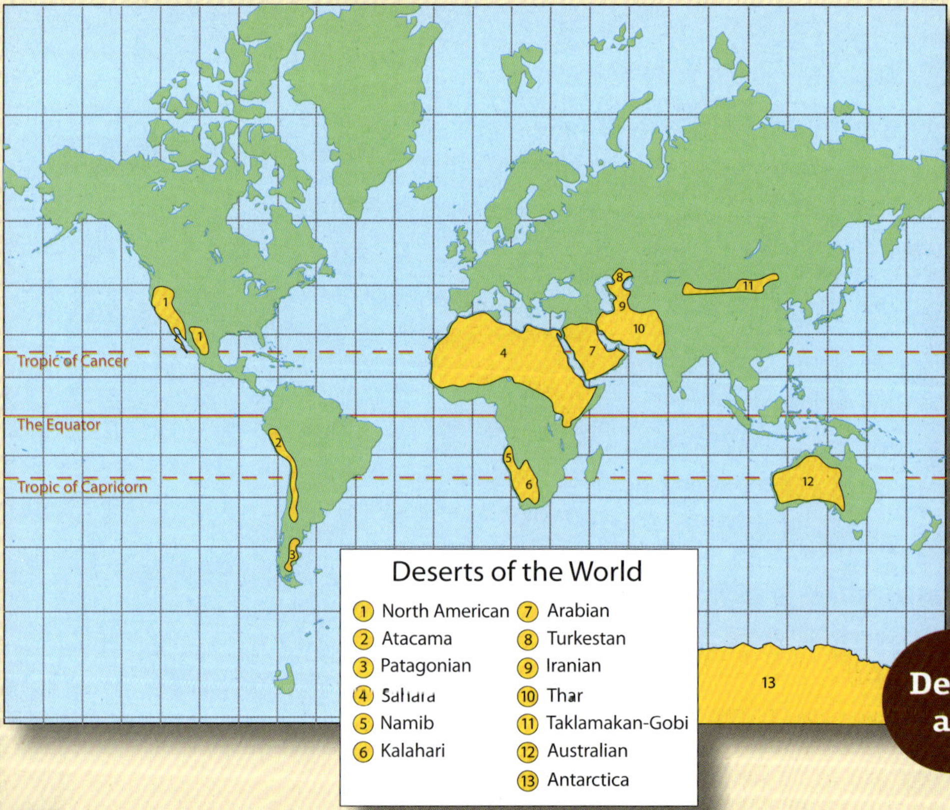

Desert ecosystems have these same pieces, too. Many have plants and animals. There is land, water, and air. Everything works together. Deserts can be filled with life.

Deserts can be found all over the world.

Biome

A desert is one of many types of **biomes** (BAHY-ohms) on planet Earth. A biome is a large area with similar plant life and climate throughout. It can contain many ecosystems. The major biomes of the world are tundra, grassland, forest, marine, freshwater, and, of course, desert.

desert pond

coyotes

The cereus cactus shown here can only bloom at night.

ladybug on a bunny ears cactus

The Sahara Desert in Africa is at a low latitude.

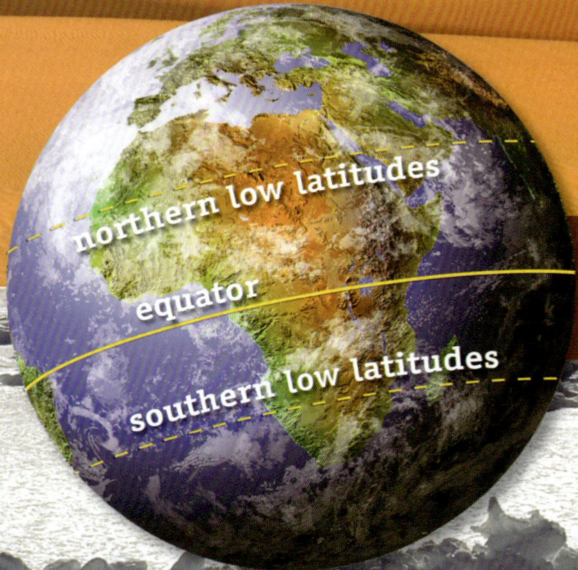

Low latitudes appear in the areas just north and south of the equator.

The Antarctic desert is at the highest latitude at the most southern point on the planet.

Deserts can be found all over the world. People often think of deserts as they do the Sahara (suh-HAIR-uh). Such deserts are found at low latitudes (LAT-i-toods). They are called **hot deserts**. They are hot, dry, and may be sandy. But deserts can be found at high latitudes as well. These are called **cold deserts**. They are often covered in snow and ice. Antarctica (ant-AHRK-ti-kuh) is the largest cold desert in the world. It is nearly covered in a thick sheet of ice.

Two other types of deserts are **semiarid** (sem-ee-AIR-id) and **coastal**. Semiarid deserts may get low rainfall. But they may get a lot of moisture from dew that forms during cold nights. Coastal deserts are found along ocean coastlines. These deserts are warm to cool. They may have short winters and long summers.

Temperature

There may be a wide range of temperatures through the day in a desert. Nights can be freezing (0°C/32°F or lower), and days can be extremely hot (49°C/120°F or higher).

Rainfall

In a desert, there is usually less than 25 centimeters (10 inches) of rain each year.

A person may wonder why deserts are important. With so little life, what good are they? They are important for a few reasons. Deserts provide places to live for certain animals and plants. They provide good sources of energy. And they are beautiful.

Some animals and plants need the **environment** (en-VIE-ruhn-muhnt) that a desert offers. In fact, the desert is a really good place for them. They do not have to compete with many other species to get what they need. The hardest job they have is finding water. But they can find it if they know where to look. Desert plants and animals know how to survive with little water.

Deserts can also provide good sources of energy. Wind is made when hot air rises and heavy cold air rushes in to take its place. Windmills can use this wind and turn it into electricity. It is a source of energy. It does not harm the environment.

Deserts are also beautiful. There may be rolling landscapes. There may be jutting rocks. There may be fields of wildflowers. There may be towering cactus under bright blue skies. These can be some of the prettiest sights around. People may travel for miles just to see a desert's beauty.

Some people think that deserts are the most beautiful places on Earth.

Modern windmills like these use wind to make electricity. At one time, windmills were the only source of energy for ranchers and farmers in the deserts.

A Big Chunk

Deserts cover a large part of the planet. Together, they make up about one-third of Earth's land surface.

Desert Animals

Animals can be found in most deserts. **Reptiles** and birds are common there. So are insects and spiders. Some **mammals** also live there. But desert life is harder for mammals than for some other animals. Most mammals cannot store the water needed to live there. There is not much shade to keep large mammals cool.

One common type of animal in a desert is a reptile. Many have adapted to desert life. For example, take the sidewinder rattlesnake. It forms its body into an S. Then it crawls sideways across the ground. But it only lets a few inches of its long body touch the ground. This keeps its belly from getting too hot on the desert floor. It is also easier to move across the sand in this way.

sidewinder rattlesnake

The chuckwalla (CHUHK-wah-luh) is a plump lizard. It is about as long as a loaf of bread. It has loose skin around its neck. It likes to have a temperature of about 40°C (105°F). It basks in the sun until it reaches that level. To protect itself, the chuckwalla climbs into cracks in rocks. Then it puffs up its body. It becomes wedged in tightly. Nothing can get to it.

Horned Lizard

Horned lizards are common in some deserts. They are about 8-15 centimeters (3-6 inches) long. Horned lizards get their name because of the tiny horns along their heads, chins, sides, and backs. The female horned lizard can lay about 30 eggs at one time!

horned lizard

chuckwalla

Birds of all sizes and types can be found in deserts. The ostrich lives in Africa. It is huge. It can weigh about 115 kilograms (250 pounds). It can grow as tall as 2.75 meters (9 feet)! A male ostrich lives with a few females. The females lay their eggs in the same nest. They work together to protect their family.

A roadrunner is a bird about .6 meters (2 feet) long. Roadrunners can fly. But they would rather walk or run. They run very fast. They run so fast that they can catch hummingbirds in the air!

Quails are smaller birds. But they are still easy to spot. Each quail has a tuft of black feathers at the top of its head. Baby quails follow their mothers in a line. Their tufts of feathers bob along with hers.

Hummingbirds are the smallest of all. They are very important to deserts. They help to carry the **pollen** (POL-uhn) from one flower to another. This lets more flowers grow. Many desert flowers depend on hummingbirds.

Lappet-Faced Vulture

The lappet-faced vulture is a common desert bird in Africa and Arabia. It is very

ostrich

roadrunner

hummingbird

quail

Desert insects and spiders are fascinating. The aphid (AF-id) is a tiny bug. It has two little tubes that stick out of its belly. It uses these to suck fluid from plants. This causes the plant's leaves to shrivel up. The aphid also releases a milky fluid from its body. Ants eat this fluid like the milk from a cow.

The queen butterfly is common in deserts. It often basks in the sun to get warm. It uses the heat of the sun to get warm enough to fly. The queen butterfly likes to feed on the milkweed plant. This plant is harmful to many animals. But it is not harmful to the queen butterfly. If a bird tries to eat the queen, the milkweed that the butterfly has eaten will make the bird sick. Birds stay away from these butterflies.

A tarantula is a large, hairy spider. It can live for 40 years! Insects are its food. It does not have to worry about water. It gets most of its water from the bodies of its prey.

Scorpions are found all over the world. They have eight legs like spiders do. But two of their legs are claws. They use the claws to catch and eat insects. But scorpions can only eat liquid. So they tear their food into tiny pieces. They get rid of anything that is not liquid.

Pupfish

It is hard to imagine a fish living in a desert, but some do! Tiny pupfish live in marshes and pools made by springs of water. The water is salty, just like ocean water.

Sonoran Desert Toad

Even though there is little water, some **amphibians** still make the desert their home. The Sonoran desert toad lives in burrows under the ground. It lays its eggs in whatever water sources it can find.

aphid

queen butterfly

tarantula

scorpion

bighorn sheep

hyena

kangaroo rat

Even though desert life can be hard for mammals, some of them live in deserts. Most mammals there are small, but some are large.

Bighorn sheep are among the largest desert mammals. They are skilled at finding pools of water. Their nimble hooves help them to climb across desert rocks and cliffs. Bighorn sheep were once nearly extinct. But the efforts of the Boy Scouts of America helped to bring back their numbers.

Another large desert animal is the hyena. It can grow to be about 1.5 meters (5 feet) long. Hyenas live in packs. They sometimes eat prey that has been killed by other animals. But they also hunt their own food.

The kangaroo rat is a common small mammal in deserts. They have long back legs like mice have. When they run, they hop like kangaroos hop.

Ships of the Desert

Camels are called the ships of the desert. They are able to live very well there. Camels can eat just about any part of any living thing, animal or plant. They can store food as fat for long periods of time. Their bodies are made so that they can live a long time without water. In this way, they do not have to compete with other animals for resources.

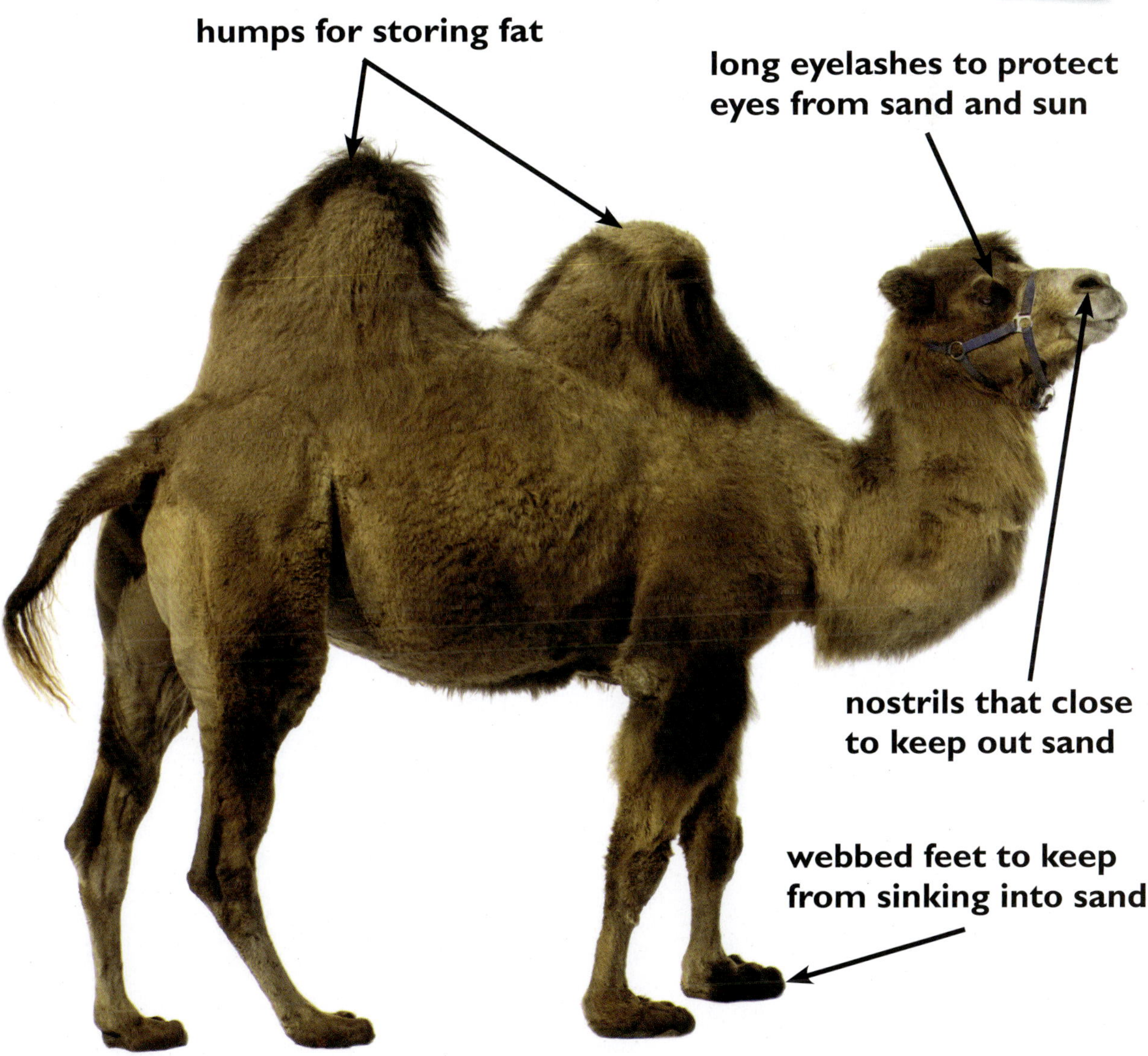

desert holly

pickleweed

wildflowers

Desert Plants

Even though there is little water, many deserts have a variety of plant life. The plants have found ways to survive. Some store water for long periods of time. Some have roots that travel deep to find water below ground. Some grow small so that they do not need much water. Some grow and bloom just briefly when water is present.

The desert holly is a hardy plant. It can live with salty water and soil, which is common in some deserts. Pickleweed also likes salty water and soil. It gets most of its water from beneath the ground.

Wildflowers can grow in sheets across a desert floor. The seeds lay in wait for rain to come. When it does, they bloom quickly. They make the desert seem to spring to life all at once.

Desert Trouble

Desert life can be quite calm. But it can be dramatic, too. Deserts are sometimes struck with raging wildfires. When there is a sudden, heavy rain, the hard ground does not easily absorb the water. This can create a flash flood across the land.

The creosote bush is common in some deserts. It has small green leaves and tiny flowers. American Indians once used it for healing. Scientists think that some creosote bushes may be thousands of years old!

The saguaro (suh-GWAHR-oh) cactus is a common desert sight. At dusk, its shadow can look like a person with arms stretched upward. The cactus stores water so that it always has what it needs. It can live for 200 years and grow to be 15 meters (50 feet) tall!

The barrel cactus also stores its water. It has a barrel shape. It is covered with ridges and pointy spines. It may wear a patch of blooming flowers at its top.

Dust Devils

If you visit a desert, you will probably see a dust devil. All a dust devil needs is dry, hot ground, a clear sky, and bright sun. Dirt and sand from the desert floor wrap in a column of hot air. It rotates like a tornado. A dust devil can grow to about 15 meters (50 feet) wide and 30 meters (100 feet) tall. Watch out!

Cactus spines are pointy and tough. They are a good protection for the cactus. Animals can be easily and painfully pricked.

The camel thorn tree grows widely across the Kalahari (kah-luh-HAHR-ee) Desert in Africa. It usually grows as a tree, but sometimes it grows as a bush. The wood of the plant is very hard and dense. People in the area once used the wood for cooking. But now the tree is **endangered**.

The most well-known part of the plant are its seed pods. They form in the shape of a crescent (KRES-uhnt) moon. They are covered in a soft gray coat. Inside are many small seeds. The seeds are packed in with a powder that is very healthy to eat. Some animals use these seeds to survive when other plants are not available.

Desert Soil

Desert soil is usually rich with nutrients. It needs only water for plants to quickly sprout and flourish.

The camel thorn tree is not named for a camel. It gets its name from the Latin name for *giraffe,* which is *camelopardus*.

The desert may look empty, but it is really full of life.

Living Together

Each part of the desert depends on other parts. The sunlight brings energy to plants. Animals eat the plants. The animals die and give nutrients to the Earth. The plants use the nutrients to grow. Water, air, and land also give living things what they need. All of this together creates a web of energy.

No part of the desert can exist without the others. Living things in the desert know how to use what the desert has to offer in order to survive. And they do not *just* survive. They live very well. The desert is their home.

Lab: What Makes an Ecosystem?

An ecosystem is made of relationships. Land, water, air, and living things live together. The living things depend on everything around them to survive. Do the lab activity on this page to learn more about ecosystems.

Materials

- paper and pen or pencil
- yarn
- tape
- reference books or the Internet

Procedure:

1. Copy the chart from this page onto your paper. Be sure to draw the chart on a large sheet of paper. It should be much larger than what you see here.
2. Write the name of the ecosystem at the top of the chart.
3. In each circle, write the name of something that belongs to that group that lives in the ecosystem.
4. Draw lines from each item, connecting it to every other item that it needs or uses or that needs or uses it.

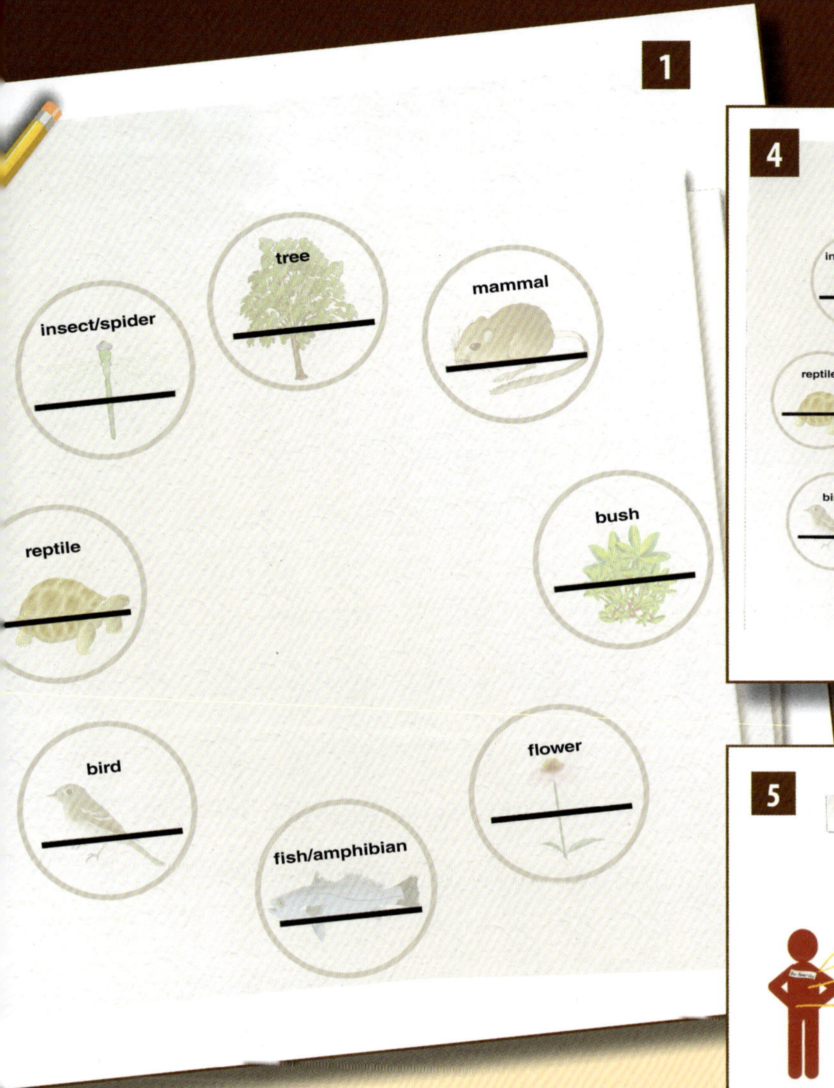

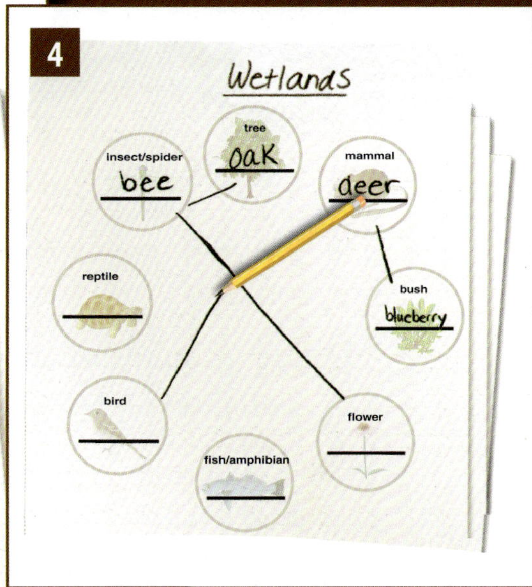

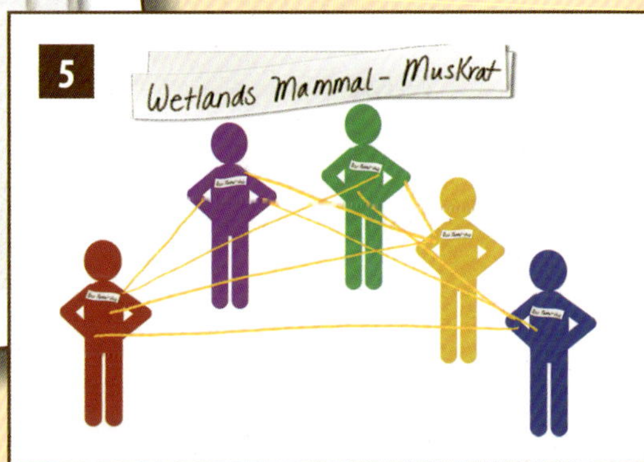

5. Now, as a class, select one of the charts that were made. You will all work together to recreate the chart in a physical way. To do it, write the key terms from the chosen chart on sentence strips and pass them out to individual students. The students now represent those key terms. Then yarn and tape can be used to connect the students. The yarn represents the lines that were connected on the chart.

6. Looking at the classroom chart, what conclusions can you make about the ecosystem? Bonus question: What part do people play in this ecosystem?

Glossary

amphibian—cold-blooded animal that lives in both water and on land

biome—complex community that is characterized by its common plants, animals, and climate

coastal desert—desert that runs along the coast of an ocean, and usually has a short winter and long summer

cold desert—high-latitude desert often covered in ice or snow

desert—area of land characterized by low rainfall

ecosystem—geographical area where plants, animals, land, air, and water all interact

endangered—in danger of becoming extinct

environment—the air, water, minerals, living things, and everything else surrounding an area or organism

hot desert—dry, sandy, low-latitude desert

mammal—warm-blooded animal that gives birth to live young

pollen—the fertilizing part of flowering plants

reptile—cold-blooded vertebrate such as a tortoise or snake

semiarid desert—desert that is somewhat more wet than other deserts, getting some level of moisture through dew and other sources

species—group of living things that share common genetic and behavioral characteristics

Index

Scientists Then and Now

Rachel Carson
(1907–1964)

Mary L. Cleave
(1947–)

Rachel Carson spent a lot of time in nature when she was a girl. She also liked to read and write stories. When she grew up, she wrote about nature. Her most famous book is called *Silent Spring*. It tells how pollution can harm living things. Rachel Carson helped people to see how important it is to take care of our planet.

Mary Cleave is an expert in many areas of science. In school, she studied biology, ecology, and engineering. She spent a lot of time after college studying animals in nature. She especially did research on the desert and its animals. Then, in 1980, she became a NASA astronaut! She flew into outer space on two different space shuttle missions.

Image Credits

Cover & p.1 sylvaine thomas/Shutterstock; p.4-5(background) Bill Lawson/Shutterstock; p.4-5(top) Litwin Photography/Shutterstock; p.4-5(bottom) Bill Lawson/Shutterstoc/Shutterstock; p.5(top) bierchen/Shutterstock; p.5(bottom) Dolor Ipsum/Flickr; p.6 Cartesia_LKPalmer p.7(top left) Lukasz Misiek/Shutterstock; p.7(top right) N. Frey Photography/Shutterstock; p.7(bottom left) Aiti/Shutterstock; p.7(bottom right) urosr/Shutterstock; p8 LKPalmer; p.8-9(top) Galyna Andrushko/Shutterstock; p.8-9(bottom) Armin Rose/Shutterstock; p.10-11 Wolfgang Staudt/Flickr; p.11 Photoroller/Shutterstock; p.12-13 Rusty Dodson/Shutterstock; p.13 David Brimm/Shutterstock; p.13(top) Rusty Dodson/Shutterstock, p.14 Julian Swanepoel/Shutterstock; p.14-15 kristian sekulicShutterstock; p.15(top right) Nelson Sirlin/Shutterstock; p.15(right center) jhaskellus/Flickr; p.15(bottom) JNStuart/Flickr; p.16 blickwinkel/Alamy; p.17(top right) xoque/Flickr; p.17(middle left) Joseph Calev/Shutterstock; p.17(middle right) Sergey Chushkin/Shutterstock; p.17(bottom left) Jens Peermann/Shutterstock; p.17(bottom right) EcoPrint/Shutterstock; p.18(top) IPK Photography/Shutterstock; p.18(middle) 7382489561/Shutterstock; p.18(bottom) Anthony Mercieca/Photo Researchers, Inc.; p.19 Eric Isselée/Shutterstock; p.20(top left) Rodney Mehring/Shutterstock; p.20(top right) jkirkhart35/Flickr; p.20(bottom) sbisson/Flickr; p.21 Shabinad/Dreamstime; p.22 Beverley Vycital/iStockphoto; p.22–23(top left) n8agrin/Flickr; p.23(top right) Anton Foltin/Shutterstock; p.23(bottom right) Daniel Gilbey/Shutterstock; p.23 (bottom left) Tan Kian Khoon/Shutterstock; p.24 Cartesia; p.24-25 Jonathan Heger/Shutterstock; p.25(left) Pkruger/Shutterstock; p.25(right) Winfried Bruenken/Wikimedia; p.26-27 Sourav and Joyeeta Chowdhury/Shutterstock; p.28-29 Nicolle Rager Fuller; p.32(left) U.S. Fish and Wildlife Service; p.32(right) NASA.